# Avaricious Aardvarks

## Fun with Alphabet Tongue Twisters and God's Amazing Creatures

**by Sandy Sheppard**
**illustrated by Joel Bower**

*Sandy Sheppard*

First paperback printing, 1998
The Standard Publishing Company, Cincinnati, Ohio. A division of Standex International Corporation
© 1994 by The Standard Publishing Company. All rights reserved. Printed in the United States of America

05    04    03    02    01    00    99    98          5    4    3    2    1

Cataloging-in-Publication data available. ISBN 0-7847-0796-0. UPC 7-07529-04254-1.
Designed by Coleen Davis

Scripture from The Bible in Today's English Version, © 1966, 1971, 1976
by the American Bible Society. Used by permission.

Curious beasts from A to Z
Fill the earth, the sky, the sea.

They jump and fly and swim and crawl;
God our Father made them all.

**Avaricious aardvarks antagonize anxious ants.**

**Big brown baboons buy bananas by the bunch.**

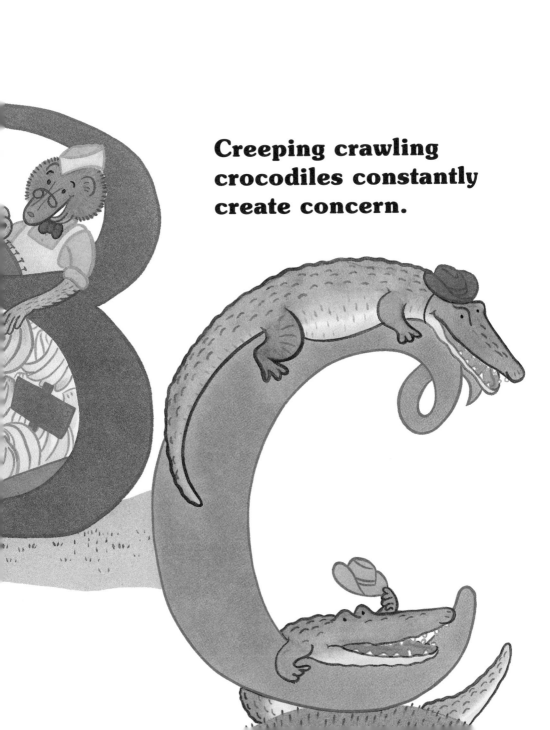

**Creeping crawling crocodiles constantly create concern.**

**Dehydrated dromedaries don't drink daintily.**

**Energetic elephants enjoy exercising endlessly.**

**Friendly frogs frolic friskily for fun.**

**Gorgeous gorillas
give glamorous gifts.**

**Huge
hungry
hippos
have
happy
holidays.**

**Intelligent iguanas
imagine interesting
insects.**

**Jolly jaguars jump joyfully in jungles.**

**Kindly
kangaroos
kiss kinfolk.**

**Listless lions lazily lap liquids.**

**Mice make mischief merrily.**

# Narwhals never need knitting needles.

Oodles of octopuses occupy oceans.

# Perceptive poodles prohibit petting porcupines.

**Quiet quails quaintly quilt.**

# Reckless rhinos run rapidly.

**Sleek seals swiftly swallow salmon steaks.**

# Terrible tigers test their trouble-making talents.

**Ugly umbrellabirds use unusual utensils.**

**Venomous vipers visit in vivid velvet vests.**

**Wealthy walruses wear waistcoats with waterproof watches.**

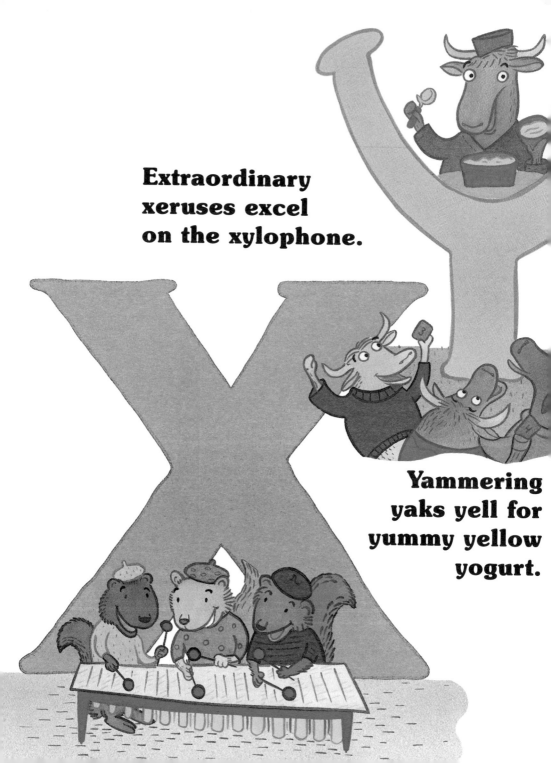

**Extraordinary xeruses excel on the xylophone.**

**Yammering yaks yell for yummy yellow yogurt.**

**Zany zebras zip zigzag zippers.**

**"Lord, the earth is filled with your creatures."**

Psalm 104:24